AF268671

Keeping Zen in the Pig Pen

ADVENTURES WITH AMARA AND HER PIGGY.

Written by: Jeenetha Kulasingam   Illustrated by: Nataliia Tymoshenko

Keeping Zen in the Pig Pen, is a work of fiction about the life of a girl named Amara and any references to other actual people or places are purely coincidental.

Copyright © 2022 Jeenetha Kulasingam.
All rights reserved. This book or any portions thereof may not be reproduced or used in any manner whatsoever without the express written permission of the author, except for the use of brief quotations in a book review.

ISBN
All rights reserved.

To Amara
My favourite girl, nothing can stop
you with piggy by your side.

To Rames, Maran and Amara
Thank you for always motivating me
to live to my fullest potential.

To Appa and Amma
You taught me that with an education
comes freedom, and I am forever
grateful for this lesson.

My name is Amara
and I am only three.
I am full of emotions
only my piggy can see!

My heart thumps loud,
I let out a "ROAR",
when my mother wipes the art
I drew on the kitchen floor.

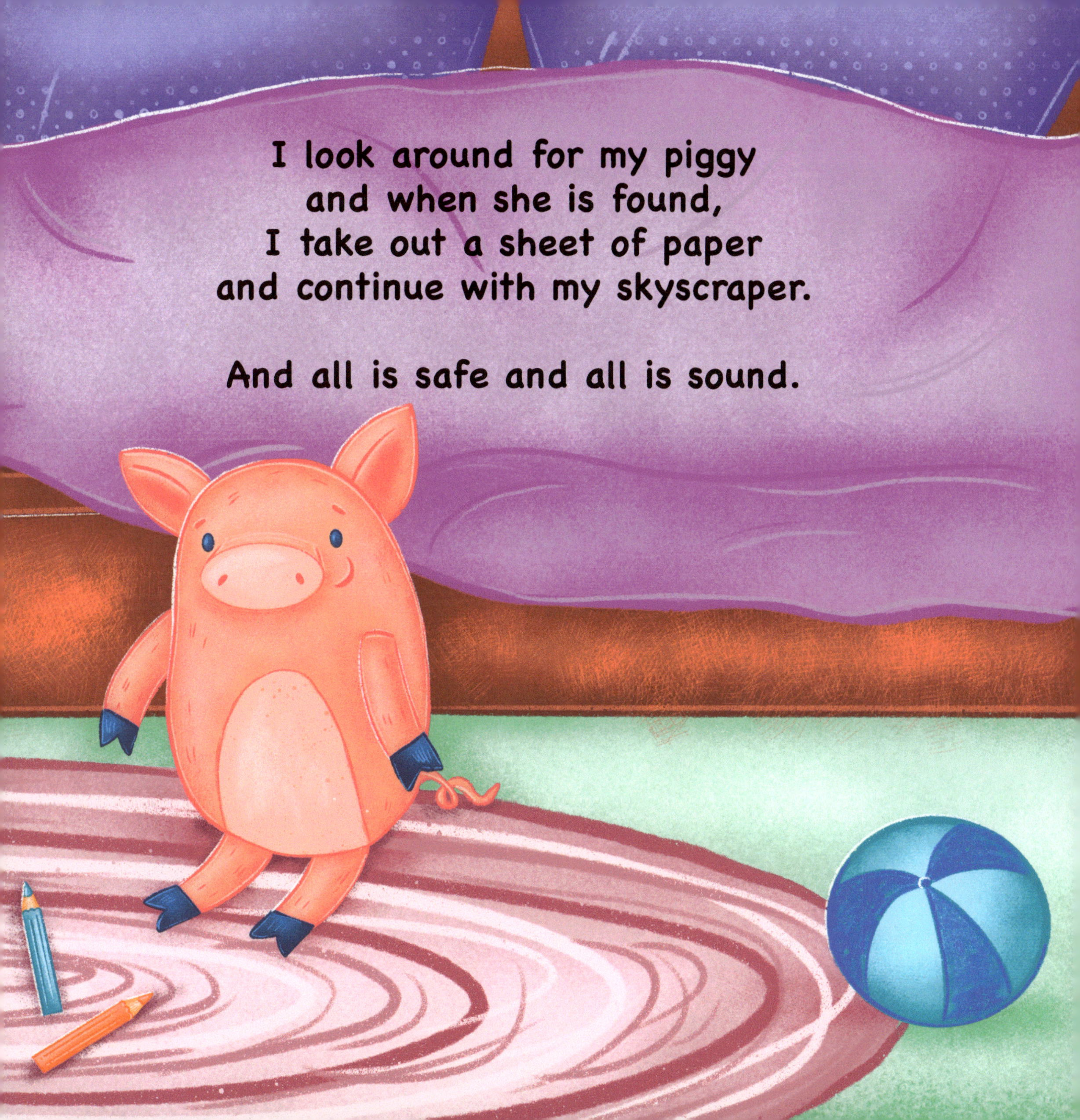

I look around for my piggy
and when she is found,
I take out a sheet of paper
and continue with my skyscraper.

And all is safe and all is sound.

"Eat your okra and soak up that vitamin C,"
mom says oh so sternly.
But it feels unpleasantly gloopy
and all too much like my icky boogie!

I look around for my piggy
and when she is found,
I close my eyes tight
and take a small bite.

And all is safe and all is sound!

"Hey Amara, want to come out with my buddies and I to play soccer?" My brother offers.
My hands and feet start to freeze.
My words are stuck in my throat with unease.

I look around for my piggy and when she is found,
she flashes a grin.
Instantly, I join my brother and friends
playing for the win!

And all is safe and all is sound.

Now it's time for bed
and dad tucks me in tight.
He says, "sweet dreams Amara
and have a good night."

With eyes wide open,
I see shadows of wolves
and snakes in motion!

I look around for my piggy
and when she is found,

I gently fall asleep
feeling safe and sound.

THE
END

www.ingramcontent.com/pod-product-compliance
Lightning Source LLC
Chambersburg PA
CBHW042142030726
47599CB00002B/586